Sigmund Brouwer

Watch Out for Joel!

Camp

D1402034

BETHANY BACKYARD®

www.bethanyhouse.com

Published by Bethany House Publishers
A Ministry of Bethany Fellowship International
11400 Hampshire Avenue South
Bloomington, Minnesota 55438
www.bethanyhouse.com

Printed in China

Library of Congress Cataloging-in-Publication Data

Brouwer, Sigmund, 1959-
   Camp craziness / by Sigmund Brouwer.
      p. cm. — (Watch out for Joel!)
Summary: At summer camp, seven-year-old Joel and his older brother, Ricky, must decide how to deal with a bully.
   ISBN 0-7642-2582-0
   [1. Camps—Fiction. 2. Bullies—Fiction. 3. Brothers—Fiction. 4. Christian life—Fiction.] I. Title.
   PZ7.B79984 Cam   2003
   [E]—dc21
                                             2002010733

Don't Be Mean!

Joel is scared of the outhouse. Then Tom plans something very mean for Joel. Can Ricky and Joel stop him, or will Tom get away with his plan?

Proverbs 14:22 says, "Those who make evil plans will be ruined. But people love and trust those who do good." Ricky and Joel want to get revenge on Tom. As you read the story, can you think of a time when you wanted revenge?

1

Joel was only seven, but he liked being at summer camp. Joel was at summer camp with his older brother, Ricky. Ricky was thirteen.

Joel liked everything at summer camp except for the outhouse.

Joel hated the outhouse.

The outhouse was smelly.

The outhouse was dark.

The outhouse had spiders and flies and other bugs.

Worst of all, Joel was afraid that he might fall down into the bottom of the outhouse. Everyone knows how terrible that would be!

Joel hated the outhouse so much that he waited as long as possible before he had to use it.

But Joel could not wait forever.

Finally, he went into the outhouse.

He held his breath as long as he could because the outhouse was smelly.

He kept his flashlight on because the outhouse was dark.

He was ready to scare away spiders and flies and other bugs.

Most of all, he was very careful not to fall into the bottom of the outhouse. Everyone knows how terrible that would be!

Joel was nearly finished in the outhouse.

Then he looked down at his feet.

He saw a big, black snake. It was crawling toward his legs!

2

A snake! A big, black snake!

In the outhouse!

Joel jumped!

Joel screamed!

Joel pulled open the door!

Joel jumped over the snake!

Joel ran out of the outhouse!

He was in such a hurry that he had time to pull up only his underwear. He did not pull up his pants. Joel fell because his pants tripped his legs.

Joel did not stop to pull his pants up all the way.

He crawled on his stomach as fast as he could. Joel was afraid the big, black snake might chase him.

Then Joel heard someone laugh.

It was a bully named Tom.

Tom laughed and laughed.

"Hey, Joel," Tom said. "It was funny to see you run away from the big, black snake in the outhouse!"

Joel stood up. He pulled his pants up all the way.

"How did you know there was a big, black snake in the outhouse?" Joel asked.

"Because I put the big, black snake in there to scare you," Tom said. "I thought it would be funny. And I was right. Best of all, I took pictures of you running away from the snake."

3

Tom showed Joel his camera.

"See?" Tom said. "Now I have pictures of you crawling away from the snake."

"I do not like that," Joel said. "I did not have time to pull my pants up all the way. People will see my underwear in the pictures."

Tom laughed and laughed.

"I know," Tom said. "That is the best part of all!"

Just then, Joel's brother, Ricky, walked up to Tom and Joel.

"What is happening?" Ricky asked.

"There was a snake in the outhouse," Joel said.

"Tom put it there. Then he took pictures as I ran from the snake."

Tom laughed and laughed.

"Yes," Tom told Ricky. "They will be very good pictures. I will show them to everyone at school."

"Please do not do that," Joel said to Tom. "I do not want my friends at school to see my underwear in the pictures."

"Do not do that," Ricky said to Tom. "He is only seven. You are fourteen. You should not be mean to him."

"What are you going to do?" Tom asked Ricky. "Take the camera from me?"

"I cannot do that," Ricky said. "You are much bigger than I am."

Tom laughed and laughed.

"You are right," Tom said. "I am much bigger. When school starts, all of Joel's friends will see the pictures of him in his underwear."

Tom walked away with the camera.

"What will we do?" Joel asked.

"I will think of something," Ricky said. "Just wait and see."

4

Just before suppertime, Ricky showed Joel what they would do to play a trick on Tom the bully.

"Look at this," Ricky said to Joel. Ricky held a small bottle. "This is hot sauce. We will pour it into a bowl of chili and give it to Tom. After Tom eats the chili, his mouth will get very, very hot. He will have to run to get lots and lots of water to drink. While he is getting water, we will go to his tent and find his camera. We will open the camera, and the light will ruin the pictures. Then no one at school will ever see the pictures of you in your underwear running away from the snake."

Joel thought of Tom the bully eating a bowl of chili with hot sauce. Joel thought of Tom the bully running and screaming for water.

"That is a good idea," Joel said. "Summer camp is fun."

So Ricky and Joel poured half a bottle of hot sauce into Tom's chili.

Joel and Ricky walked over to Tom.

"Here you are," Ricky said to Tom. "Here is your chili for supper."

Tom put a spoon in the bowl of chili. Tom got ready to take a big bite.

5

Tom lifted his big spoon of chili.

Then John walked up to Joel and Ricky and Tom.

"Hello," John said. He was the camp leader. He was bald. He wore glasses. "Can I have that chili?"

"No!" Joel said.

"No!" Ricky said.

"Yes," Tom said.

John took a big, big bite. John quickly ate the whole bowl of chili.

Then John's face turned red.

Then the top of John's bald head turned red.

Then John yelled and screamed for water. His glasses fell off. John ran for water as fast as he could.

"Oh no," Joel said.

"Oh no," Ricky said.

Camp leader John was very mad at Joel and Ricky. He made them wash and dry all the dishes that night.

6

There were a lot of dishes. An hour later, Joel and Ricky were still washing and drying them.

Tom laughed and laughed.

"You tried to get me back," he said as he watched Joel and Ricky wash and dry the dishes. "But it didn't work."

Tom took out his camera.

He took pictures of Joel and Ricky as they washed and dried the dishes.

Tom laughed and laughed.

"This is funny," Tom said. "I have pictures of Joel in his underwear as he ran from the snake.

Now I have pictures of you washing and drying the dishes. I can show everybody at school what you had to do because you put hot sauce in the chili."

"Please do not do that," Joel said to Tom. "I do not want my friends at school to see my underwear in the pictures. I do not want my friends at school to see what happened because we put hot sauce in the chili."

Tom laughed and laughed.

"There is nothing you can do to get my camera," Tom said. "I am going to take it with me everywhere I go."

Tom walked away with his camera.

"What will we do?" Joel asked.

"I don't know," Ricky said. "I am afraid that when school starts, Tom will show all your friends the pictures of you in your underwear."

7

The next day, Joel had to use the outhouse again.

"I am afraid of the outhouse," Joel said to Ricky. "I hate the outhouse."

The outhouse was smelly. The outhouse was dark. The outhouse had spiders and flies and other bugs.

Worst of all, Joel was afraid that sometime he might fall down into the bottom of the outhouse. Everyone knows how terrible that would be!

"Yes," Ricky said. "I understand why you hate the outhouse."

"And what if there is a big, black snake in there?" Joel asked. "What if I open the door of the outhouse and the snake jumps out at me?"

Ricky thought about it.

Ricky smiled.

"I have an idea," Ricky said. "Your older brother will show you how to open the outhouse door. If there is a snake in the outhouse, we will scare the snake!"

Joel followed Ricky to the outhouse.

"Shhh!" Ricky said to Joel. "If there is a snake in there, we want to surprise it!"

"How will we do that?" Joel whispered.

"Let your older brother show you," Ricky said.

Joel followed Ricky right up to the door of the outhouse.

"Ready?" Ricky whispered to Joel.

"Ready," Joel whispered to Ricky.

"Hiiiiii-yaaaaa!" Ricky screamed. He kicked open the door as hard as he could.

The door slammed open.

And someone inside screamed!

8

The screams and yells kept coming from inside the outhouse.

"That does not sound like a snake," Joel said.

"You are right," Ricky said. "It sounds like a person. Someone must have been inside the outhouse, and we did not know it."

"Oh no," Joel said. "What if it is camp leader John?"

"I hope not," Ricky said. "Then we will have to wash and dry dishes until we are very, very old."

The screams and yells kept coming from inside the outhouse.

Joel and Ricky stepped inside the outhouse. But they could not see anyone.

"Oh no," Joel said.

"Oh no," Ricky said.

The screams and yells kept coming from inside the outhouse. From the very bottom of the outhouse.

"Help me," someone shouted from the bottom of the outhouse. "I am stuck down here!"

It was Tom the bully.

When Ricky had kicked open the door, the door hit Tom and knocked him to the bottom of the outhouse. And everyone knows how terrible that would be!

"Help me," Tom the bully shouted again from the bottom of the outhouse. "I am stuck down here!"

9

Joel and Ricky found a rope. They returned to the outhouse.

They threw the rope down to the bottom of the outhouse.

Tom climbed out of the bottom of the outhouse. He was very, very dirty.

"What are you doing?" he asked Ricky.

"Say cheese," Ricky said.

Ricky had a camera of his own. He took pictures of Tom, who was very, very dirty from the bottom of the outhouse.

"There," Ricky said. "Now we can trade. If you

give me the pictures of Joel in his underwear, I will give you these pictures."

"No," Tom said. "I can't make you that trade."

"Do you want your friends at school to see you coming out of an outhouse looking like this?" Ricky said. Tom was very, very dirty from the bottom of the outhouse.

"No," Tom said. "But I don't have my camera. I said I would take it everywhere with me. I took it into the outhouse. It fell into the bottom with me. I will never find the camera."

"Oh," Joel said. "So now you can't show my friends at school the pictures of me in my underwear?"

"No," Tom said.

"I still have pictures of you," Joel said. "But I won't show them to anyone. Because I remember how much I didn't want you to show pictures of me in my underwear."

Tom was so happy, he tried to hug Joel.

"Yuck," Joel said. Joel pushed Tom away. "Not when you smell like an outhouse!"

A Lesson About Revenge

In *Camp Craziness*, Ricky and Joel don't like how Tom is treating them, so they make plans to get back at him.

People are sometimes mean to us. We might want to do something mean to them in return. But God wants us to act differently and treat people kindly, even when they are mean to us.

To Talk About

1. How does it feel when someone is mean to you?
2. What can you do to *not* be mean in return?
3. What can you do to show God's love to others?

> "Forget about the wrong things people do to you. You must not try to get even. Love your neighbor as you love yourself."
> Leviticus 19:18

Award-winning author Sigmund Brouwer inspires kids to love reading. From WATCH OUT FOR JOEL! to the ACCIDENTAL DETECTIVES series (full of stories about Joel's older brother, Ricky), Sigmund writes books that kids want to read again and again. Not only does he write cool books, Sigmund also holds writing camps and classes for more than ten thousand children each year!

You can read more about Sigmund, his books, and the Young Writer's Institute on his Web site, *www.coolreading.com*.